We cannot cho

(

the world can be forever changed.

Adopting Joy:

A homeless pup finds love and happiness

Karen Dubs

This book is based on a true story and is dedicated to my precious rescue pups Stella, Luna, and Leo and to the thousands of other homeless pups who are waiting for someone to give them the second chance they deserve.

Preface

Hello! My name is Stella. I am a rescue pup who was once homeless and hungry in Louisiana and now living my dream life in the pretty Maryland countryside with my adopted sister and brother, Luna and Leo.

My adopted momma reminds me how brave I was, and how special and perfect I am. She says my scars and imperfections are what make me so beautiful. One of her greatest joys is adopting rescue pups and watching them transform from skinny and scared, to healthy and happy. I didn't understand why until we adopted Luna and Leo and I watched them transform in just a few weeks.

I would like to share my story for when you might feel scared, hopeless, imperfect, left out, or completely alone in the world. Trust me—if I have found my way, so can you!

Chapter 1

Life In Louisiana

I was born in Louisiana. Although my fur momma always tried to reassure me and my siblings that we were special, I always worried I wasn't pretty enough, smart enough, brave enough, or perfect enough for anyone to ever love me, except for my momma of course.

I have the stocky body of a miniature pit bull, the sweet eyes of a cocker spaniel, and the short legs of a Yorkshire terrier.

I was a mutt that no one wanted. But at least I had my momma, and she loved me.

"Pure breed dogs aren't the only pups that are beautiful ," Momma said. "True beauty is about what's in your heart."

On a warm spring day, I woke up scared, hungry and alone in the woods. Somehow I had lost my fur momma. I spent the next few weeks surviving on dirty puddles of water and eating whatever scraps of food I could find. As the days passed, my golden fur became coarse and dull, my body scrawny and scraggly, my eyes tired and hollow, and I had fleas and worms—yuk. It was lonely and awful, but at least I had fresh air, peace, and quiet in the Louisiana countryside.

One day, several men chased me, caught me in a net and hauled me to a place called a shelter, where I was poked, prodded, inspected, injected, and given a flea bath. I have hated baths ever since that day. Then they shoved me into a cage surrounded by barking and crying dogs.

I didn't know what the other dogs had done wrong, but clearly, I was not supposed to be there. I didn't do anything wrong!

Adopting Joy

Even though I was surrounded by dozens of other dogs, I felt very alone and scared. It was the worst day of my life... or so I thought.

Chapter 2

The Search Begins

Over a thousand miles away in Maryland, a man and a woman wept as they buried the ashes of their beloved dog under a Weeping Redbud tree. "Rest in peace, sweet pup," they whispered as they sprinkled her ashes into the earth. "We'll never find another pup like Kacy."

That night, the man could not sleep because he no longer had his pup by his side.

The couple felt very sad. They greatly missed their beloved pup and wanted her back. Because they loved her so much, they wanted another dog of the same breed. But when they heard about the millions of rescue dogs in shelters around the country, they opened their minds and hearts to saving a pup instead of buying one.

And so their search began...

Chapter 3

Finding Gratitude And Faith

The shelter was very noisy. My fellow inmates were confused as they cried, barked, and trembled with fear. It was mayhem for a shy country girl like me who enjoys nature and quiet time.

In the months before I lost Momma, she taught me about finding gratitude and faith even in the worst of circumstances.

"Gratitude makes us appreciate the simple things in life," she said. "You can *always* find something to be grateful for."

I tried to focus my energy on the good things: I was safe, and I didn't have to search for food or drink from dirty puddles of water anymore.

Soon a smiling lady with kind eyes gave me food and water. "Eat up, pup," she said as she patted my head. Yes, I felt grateful, but boy, did I need to stretch my legs! I had been cramped up in the small crate all day.

Days crawled along. Weeks passed. Some of the other pups left with families. I wanted to feel happy for them, but instead, I thought—*What's wrong with me? Why didn't anyone pick me?*

New pups arrived daily. They always looked scared and confused. I tried to reassure them that everything would be okay. Momma taught me to be kind to others.

"The kindness you share will come back to you," she said.

I knew Momma was right, yet I wondered why it was taking so long for my good actions to return to me.

Chapter 4

Losing Hope

Months passed. I wanted to get out of the crate and run. I missed snuggling in the sun with my momma and playing with my siblings. I missed feeling the grass under my paws, smelling fresh air, and listening to the sounds of nature.

I fell asleep and dreamt of a woman taking me for a long walk on a trail in the woods. It was heavenly. But then I woke up in my cage, once again surrounded by barking and crying dogs. Darn, it was only a dream but seemed so real.

I began to lose hope. *What if I had to live the rest of my life in a cage in this noisy, crowded shelter?*

A few days later, two ladies walked around the shelter, eyeing up the dogs in each cage. I gave them my best, sad sap look. The ladies took out ten of us for an extra-long playtime. It was the most fun I had had in weeks! We ran and played and sniffed each other to say hello. For a few minutes, I forgot I was in a shelter.

After playing, the ladies loaded me and several other dogs into a big van. I didn't know why they took us or where we were going, but I figured it would be better than where we were!

I felt hopeful.

We arrived at our destination where one of the ladies wrapped a purple "Adopt Me" vest around my waist. Dozens of people walked by and looked at me.

"Awww, poor skinny puppy," one lady said.

"Is that a mutt?" another one asked.

I tried so hard to behave and stand out so someone would pick me.

A few more of my friends left with families that day, but no one wanted me.

Adopting Joy

I was so sad My heart sank as the lady put me into the van and headed back to the shelter.

The worst feeling in the world is thinking nobody loves or wants you.

Chapter 5

A New Friend

The next day, a nice lady visited the shelter. She then took me to her house and gave me a long overdue bath. *Ugh, not another bath!*

I made friends with Katie, the cat.

It was wonderful to feel grass under my paws, the sun on my face, and to run and play in a yard. I even had a stick to chew and a cozy, clean blanket in my crate.

Momma was right—it's nice to be grateful for the little things.

The lady even let me curl up beside her on the couch to watch the summer

Olympics. As she pet my golden fur, she said, "Aha, I know! I'm going to name you Missy after the Olympic gold medalist swimmer, Missy Franklin."

I was so happy… I finally had a home and a name!

That night I smiled as I fell asleep on my clean, comfy blanket. Ahhh, peace and quiet. I snoozed for a long time. I dreamt of being curled up on a couch with a nice man, which was odd since I was afraid of men. But this man seemed different. I wasn't afraid of him at all.

When I woke up, Katie told me the bad news. The nice lady was only my foster mom. This house was not my forever home—only a temporary stop.

My head slumped, and my heart hurt. I was trying so hard to get potty trained, sit like a good girl, and learn my manners. Why didn't the nice lady want to keep me?

"It's not you," said Katie. "Don't take it personally. We've fostered dozens of dogs to help them get adopted. If we keep you, there won't be room to help another homeless doggie."

"Oh. You mean I still have a chance at finding a forever home?" I asked.

"Oh, yes," Katie said. "Don't give up now. You've come this far!"

"But how much longer will it take?" I asked.

"Well, I can't say for sure, but I know that timing is always perfect. Somehow you'll end up exactly where you are supposed to be."

Katie, the cat, sounded like Momma with her talk of faith and patience.

Chapter 6

Saving One Dog

In Maryland, the couple was frustrated looking for a rescue pup to adopt. It was taking longer than they had expected. They had their heart set on "the perfect dog," one exactly like the pup that had died.

The woman went to a yoga class to lift her spirits. (Yoga always made her feel better.) After class, one of her friends suggested she should 'just buy a dog!' The friend said, "It's much easier, plus you know exactly what you're getting, instead of damaged goods."

"But why create more puppies when there are thousands of dogs already born, waiting in shelters for their second chance?" the woman replied.

"Buying a dog is safer," the friend said. "Wouldn't you like to have a cute little Chiweenie or cockapoo instead of some recycled garbage dog? Or what about a Labradoodle or Goldendoodle? They're perfect, and they don't shed."

"I think perfect is overrated. Besides, yoga means *unity*, and that *all* living beings deserve our compassion and love."

"Well, you can't save the world," the friend said. "And you could have a dog today if you went to a pet store."

"No, I can't save the world, you're right," the woman agreed. "But the least I can do is save one dog. For every dog bought from a puppy mill or pet store, another dog in a shelter doesn't get a second chance. And just so you know, all those breeds you named are simply fancy names for a mutt anyway." And she walked away.

On the drive home, the woman felt more determined than ever to adopt a mutt. She didn't understand how good people, like her friend, were so clueless about the importance of not supporting puppy mills and pet stores. She thought about the millions of dogs sitting in a shelter at that very moment, scared and alone, because someone bought them but didn't commit to their care. It made her heart hurt, and she knew she could make a difference, at least for one dog.

Chapter 7

What About Missy?

That night, the woman cried. Her husband reassured her that everything would work out. "Don't give up now! We're getting so close," he said, as they scrolled through adoption websites. "One of these doggies is going to win the lottery and have the best life ever with us."

Before she went to bed, the woman completed one more application online for a scraggly little pup named Missy in Louisiana. She saw something in the dog's eyes she immediately recognized—an expression of hope and faith, mixed with despair and fear. She knew those feelings well after burying her beloved Kacy.

The next day the woman received a phone call. She and her husband were approved to adopt Missy! In fact, the rescue organization had a van full of adopted pups traveling through Maryland on their way to New England to deliver to their forever homes. The van could make a stop in Baltimore County to drop off Missy before heading north to Massachusetts to drop off the remaining dogs.

"Missy can be on her way here tomorrow!" the woman exclaimed to her husband.

"Tomorrow!?" the man said. "Adopt a dog we've never met? That's crazy!"

"Yes, it's crazy," his wife said. "A blind date adoption with a little yellow doggie from Louisiana. It's a leap of faith!" As she took a walk on the nature trail that morning, the woman sent positive energy to Missy far away. "Hang in there pup," she thought. She smiled as she imagined Missy by her side on the walking trail.

Chapter 8

Happy Tears

Missy's foster mother was acting strangely, rushing around and crying. Missy overheard her speaking with Katie; something about "happy tears."

"What are happy tears?" Missy asked the cat.

Katie took a big breath, "Well, there's good news, and there's bad news. Which would you like to hear first?"

"I like happy endings, so let's do the bad news first!"

"Okay," Katie said. "The bad news is... it's time for us to say goodbye."

"Goodbye? But why? I like it here!"

I almost cried, then I noticed Katie grinning from cat ear to cat ear. "Because the good news is… you got a forever home!"

Chapter 9

Places to Go And People To Know

The next day—more poking, prodding, inspections, injections, and another dreaded bath. I tried to be brave, but I was shaking from head to tail. How could I be brave when I felt so scared?

"Being brave isn't about being fearless," Momma once told me. "It's about doing what scares you most. That's where the greatest joys are in life."

So, I sadly said goodbye to my friend Katie. "Good luck, Missy!" she said. "Have a good trip!"

I didn't own a thing: no bed, no toys, no blanket. My only possession was an old red harness covered with masking tape with the name "Missy" scribbled on it in black magic marker. Yet I had faith and hope.

I remembered Momma's words—"Life isn't about collecting things to look cool or brag to your friends. True happiness is being content with what you have already."

That sounded good in theory, but I was pretty sure I'd be happier with a family and a bed. I took Momma's words of wisdom to heart and was grateful for my red harness covered in masking tape. It meant someone was waiting for me!

My foster mom dropped me off with nine other rescue mutts. It was time to begin our long journey from Louisiana to Maryland. I was overwhelmed with excitement—and anxiety!

I remembered one of Momma's favorite quotes—"The journey of a thousand miles begins with a single step." So, feeling a mix of hope and fear, I took a deep breath and hopped in the van.

I heard the driver say the trip would take three days and over 18 hours of driving. Along the route, we'd make stops in Mississippi, Tennessee, South Carolina, North Carolina, West Virginia, and Virginia, with overnight stays for two nights. "Buckle up, passengers!" he said. "We have places to go and people to know."

The ride wasn't bad. Mostly it was boring, but my fellow pups and I made the best of it—we napped a lot.

I was handed off to nice strangers at every stop. During one leg of the journey, I sat in the front seat. How fun to watch the world pass by and feel my ears flopping in the breeze!

We drove through the night, on winding back roads and highways, up and down mountains, and over many bridges. We'd stop on occasion for potty breaks and to stretch our legs.

My traveling companions became anxious and impatient. "Are we there yet?" they asked again and again.

Their nervous energy was affecting me. It was a hard journey, but I stayed positive while remembering Momma's words of wisdom, "An important part of a dog's job is to teach humans about patience, but first, we must learn it ourselves."

I took another deep breath, counted to five, and exhaled. I closed my eyes and drifted off into my favorite dream—walking on a nature trail in the woods with a woman who loved me more than anyone else had ever loved me. This time my dream took a new turn... I was snuggled up and snoozing with a man on a comfy couch by a warm fire. It was lovely.

In Maryland, the man and woman shopped for a dog bed, chew toys, blankets, a collar, and a leash for Missy. They also bought the best puppy food they could find. They anxiously awaited updates about the journey on the animal rescue's Facebook page and giggled with excitement when they saw a picture of Missy sitting in the front seat, ears flopping in the wind.

"She's on her way to us!" the woman said. "We've never met, but I love her already."

"This pup has won the lottery," the man said. "She doesn't know it yet, but we're going to make all of her dreams come true."

Chapter 10

What If They Don't Like Me?

We had been on the road for three days. I met so many nice strangers, and we stopped in so many towns, I began to lose track. This time we had a female driver. She told us about her rescue pups and how she liked to volunteer to help others reach their forever homes.

"Giving back gives me great joy," she said.

It's funny how Momma, Katie, and these volunteers all seemed to think alike. I wondered what the world would be like if there were more generous, kind eople who cared about homeless, misfit pups like me and my traveling companions.

"Welcome to Maryland , kids!" the driver announced. "Just a few more miles before some of you meet your new families and then the rest will travel on to New England."

I instantly felt butterflies in my belly. After months in the shelter, weeks in foster care, and days on the road, the moment was finally here to meet my family. But I felt worried. *What if the people don't like me?*

Meanwhile, the couple anxiously waited to meet Missy, the pup from Louisiana. A van pulled up and there she was… Missy had made it! Their new pup bounced around with joyful, springy legs, and licked her family to say hello.

"Hello, Missy," the man said. "I am your new poppa, and I'm very happy to meet you."

I will admit I was a bit nervous when the man scooped me up (remember, I didn't trust most men); yet he had such a gentle touch, I knew immediately he was different. I could trust him.

"Hi, sweet girl. I bet you'd love to stretch your legs and go for a walk," the woman said. "Let's get you home and give you a bath." *Oh boy. Again with a bath.*

That night, after I was washed and had a full belly, I slept better than I had in months. I once again dreamt of walking on a beautiful path in the woods with a woman and then snuggling up for an afternoon nap with a man. This time, I recognized the man and woman in my dream!

Chapter 11

Dreams Can Come True

The next morning when I woke up, my new momma said, "Good morning, precious pup. I bet you're hungry! We have an important ceremony, and then we'll celebrate with a walk."

Then the most magical thing happened. My new momma knelt in front of me, took my paw, and said, "For richer or poorer, in sickness and in health, 'til death do us part... you have your forever home, sweet girl." She then kissed my forehead.

She gave me a big bowl of the best food I had ever tasted. "Eat up, pup," she said. "We're going for a walk. After that, Poppa plans to snuggle with you for an afternoon nap."

I couldn't believe my eyes when I saw the path in the woods. It was exactly like the one in my dreams! "I hope you like to walk," Momma said, "because we'll be coming to this nature trail almost every day."

It turns out my stubby little legs were perfect for walking, running, and even catching a frisbee four feet in the air! Every day, I began to discover talents I never knew I had.

Chapter 12

Winning The Lottery

Momma and Poppa loved me very much. I could feel it—and it was the most amazing feeling in the world.

"You are the most beautiful pup I have ever seen," Momma said. Poppa added, "I was wrong when I said this pup won the lottery. The truth is, *we are the ones* who won. She may be a mutt, but she is absolutely perfect."

I never believed in a million years I would hear those words.

Chapter 13

Little Star

Little by little, my tired eyes began to twinkle, my scraggly coat felt softer, and my star-like personality shined brighter.

My new parents decided to rename me. "Let's call her Stella," Momma said. "It means 'little star' and fits her perfectly."

People on the trail asked, "What kind of dog is that? She's gorgeous." As I smiled proudly, Momma answered, "She's a one-of-a-kind rescue mutt. You should visit the shelter to rescue one."

One day on the trail we passed one of Momma's yoga friends with her little girl. "I see you finally gave up and bought a dog. She's gorgeous," the lady said as she petted my head. "Is she a Jack Russell?"

"Nope." Momma smiled. "She's a rescue mutt. As I mentioned in yoga a few weeks ago, I was determined to save a dog instead of buy one."

"Oh, maybe I was wrong! I thought rescue dogs were all mean or misfits." The lady looked shocked. Her little girl beamed, "Mommy, mommy, let's get a rescue mutt!"

"Rescue dogs are like any living creature," Momma replied. "They just need love and someone to give them a chance for their true beauty to shine."

Chapter 14

A New Sister And Best Friend

One day, Momma and Poppa took me to an adoption event where we met another little pup. Like me, this pup was homeless, scared and skinny. So we adopted her right there on the spot! Now I had a little sister and a new best friend.

We named her Luna since Momma loves a full moon, and because *Stella Luna* is one of Momma's favorite children's books. It's a story about a baby bat that lost her mother. In her search to find her mom, she met many nice strangers and discovered her truest self. It was a story that Luna and I could both relate to. So, Stella and Luna it was. We were a team.

Momma took Luna's paw to perform the same sweet ceremony she had for me: "For richer or poorer, in sickness and in health, 'til death do us part... you have your forever home, sweet girl."

Luna and I were happier than we could ever have imagined. We did yoga with Momma in the morning, we ate plenty of veggies from the garden, and took long walks on the trail. We wrestled, played, and chased each other in the yard, and we snuggled and snoozed with Poppa. Life was even better than I had dreamt. It was perfect.

Chapter 15

Can We Keep Him?

Momma decided to train for a 5K race to raise money for other rescue animals, so of course, Luna and I helped Momma with her training runs and fundraising. "Giving back is important," she said. "Millions of dogs just like you end up in shelters every year. We must do what we can to help."

Luna and I agreed. We remembered how scary it was to be homeless and to feel unwanted. It hurt us deeply to know other dogs were still suffering.

On a beautiful, crisp fall morning, Momma ran her race, and Poppa took us to the local farmer's market. Momma met up with us after her run. Next, a spunky little pup walked over to say hello.

"Looks like he fits right in with your crew," said the woman walking the pup. "He just arrived from Texas and needs a home," she added. It turns out the woman was his foster mom, and she brought the little guy to the market to meet other dogs and people.

Stella and I looked up at Momma, pleading with our puppy eyes. "Can we keep him?"

Poppa picked up the little guy, and the pup rested his head on Poppa's shoulder.

And just like that, we had a little brother.

We named him Leo because, although he's a little fellow, he has the spirit of a courageous lion. He made it through Hurricane Harvey in Texas and somehow lost his family. Like me, he bravely traveled over a thousand miles through six states to find his forever home.

Momma did the ceremony for Leo: For richer or poorer, in sickness and in health, 'til death do us part ... you have your forever home, sweet boy," and she kissed Leo on his little head. We took a celebratory walk on the nature trail together... three misfit mutts in a perfect little pack. We were a real family.

Chapter 16

Perfectly Imperfect

Now, every day, the three of us run and play, snuggle, and snooze. Each of us is perfectly imperfect and grateful for our second chance. Against all odds, and with much courage, faith, and help from kind strangers, we made it to our forever home! We are now happy, healthy, and free.

We pray other pups like us get the second chances they deserve to live a full life. We hope more people realize how rewarding it is to adopt a rescue pup and to witness the transformation that comes when a pup receives the love and care they deserve.

Thank you for allowing me to share my story. If you are considering adding a dog to your family, please visit your local shelter before shopping for a dog. Like Momma always says, "You can't buy happiness … but you can adopt joy."

May all things be happy and well.

~ a Metta prayer

Rescue Statistics from www.ASPCA.org

- Approximately 6.5 million companion animals enter US animal shelters nationwide every year. Of those, approximately 3.3 million are dogs, and 3.2 million are cats. The number of dogs and cats entering shelters has declined from 7.2 million in 2011.

- Each year, approximately 1.5 million shelter animals are euthanized (a significant decline from 2.6 million in 2011). The decline can be partially explained by an increase in the percentage of animals adopted, and an increase in the number of stray animals successfully returned to their owners.

- Approximately 3.2 million shelter animals are adopted each year

We are clearly on the right path, but there is more work to be done in this area. Homeless animals are counting us. Make a difference by volunteering, adopting, donating and supporting your national and local shelters. Reach out to your local shelter today.

Be part of the "Adopt, Don't Shop" movement

Many people complain that it's too hard to adopt a dog. There is some paperwork and a background check, but finding an available dog that's a match for your family is easier than you might think. There are millions for dogs available of all breeds and sizes. While it's true, adopting can take a little more time and effort, the payoff is huge. You may even be like me and put a "who saved who" magnet for your car.

Often, the fastest and best way to find an animal to adopt is to visit your local shelter, attend an adoption event and follow rescue organizations on social media. Contact your local shelter ... and save a life!

Adoption Resources

The American Society for the Prevention of Cruelty to Animals (www.ASPCA.org)

The Humane Society of the United States (www.humanesociety.org)

www.Petfinder.com

www.adoptapet.com

www.trurescue.org

Discussion Questions for *Adopting Joy*:

1) What did Stella's dog mom, foster mom and adopted mom all have in common?

2) Why did Missy feel so sad and alone?

3) What was the significance of the ceremony and vows that Stella's adopted mom said to each pup?

4) Why were Stella's adopted parents so determined to rescue a dog?

5) What trait did Stella practice on her long trip? Why is this trait important?

6) How did Stella overcome her fears? What happened when she did something outside of her comfort zone?

7) What gave Stella her greatest joy? Why?

8) For what was Stella most grateful?

9) What did Stella, Luna, and Leo have in common?

10) What are you grateful for? How can you adopt joy today?

About the Author

 Karen Dubs is a yoga teacher, health coach, and rescue dog advocate. She and her husband and her three rescue pups Stella, Luna, and Leo live in Baltimore County, Maryland. She loves teaching yoga fundraiser classes to raise money for local shelters. You can follow Stella, Luna, and Leo on their Instagram page www.instagram.com/stellalunaleo_rescuepups

If you are a yoga teacher, please consider offering a yoga fundraiser class to support your local animal shelter. Have participants donate money to attend class as well as old blankets, towels and yoga mats for the animal shelters. To raise additional funds, you can purchase copies of this book at wholesale pricing by contacting the author at karen@flexiblewarrior.com

Part of the proceeds of this book will be donated to support animal rescue organizations.

Acknowledgments

A heartfelt THANK YOU to the thousands of rescue workers, volunteers, and fosters who go above and beyond to save millions of dogs and cats each year. Special thanks to Kat Soul who is not only a talented cover artist specializing in animal art, but she was also Leo's foster momma and has personally fostered and saved dozens of dogs.

Shout out to the millions of people who make the important choice to adopt instead of shop for a companion animal. Buying a dog may be easier, but anyone who has adopted knows the extra layer of joy and unconditional love that comes with saving a life. We are on the right path, and together we are making a difference in millions of lives each year. Eventually, our shelters will be empty if all pet owners spay and neuter and more people adopt instead of shop.

Thank you to my grandma who took in homeless dogs and cats in Baltimore city for as long as I can remember. Her beloved rescue dog "Hey Boy" inspired me and everyone in our family to open our hearts to homeless animals. Her faithful rescue cat, Katie, scored big when she found my grandma and went from being homeless in Baltimore city to relocating to the small town of Hanover, PA. My grandma's compassion laid the foundation for me, and continues to be a huge part of my love of all animals... from squirrels and birds, to cats and dogs.

Shout out to my seven year old niece Rylea for her editorial assistance and for carrying the family torch and love for all living things from insects and birds to squirrels and dogs.

Huge hugs and heartfelt thanks to Bonnie Blue Rescue in Virginia, who saved Stella, Happy Hounds Homeward Bound in Hanover, PA, who saved Luna, and Tru Rescue in Cockeysville, MD, who saved Leo.

Much gratitude to everyone at BARCS, Maryland's largest animal shelter and adoption center, who take in over 11,000 animals a year (yes, that's one shelter in one city). BARCS has made huge strides, not only saving thousands of animals a year, but in making it cool to adopt instead of shop for a pet.

Special thanks to the cover artist Kat Soul, who in addition to being a talented artist and musician, also happens to be Leo's foster mom. Momma Kat has personally foster cared and successfully rehomed dozens of rescue pups. It's people like Kat who make the world a better place.

Thank you to Suzanne Molino Singleton for your friendship and editorial assistance. You gave me the nudge and inspiration I needed to make this book a reality.

Thanks to the writer's group at Baltimore County Public Library Hereford branch for welcoming me into your group, taking the time to read my story, and offer me helpful support and honest feedback.

Lastly, thank you to my husband who swears if we ever do win the lottery, we'll buy a big farm, save thousands of more dogs, and make it cool to "adopt instead of shop" for a dog.

16601320R00043

Made in the USA
Middletown, DE
24 November 2018